U0022393

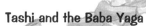

Tashi and the Baba Yaga
© Text, Anna Fienberg and Barbara Fienberg 1998
© Illustrations, Kim Gamble 1998
First published in 1998 by Allen & Unwin Pty Ltd., Australia

大喜說故事系列

Tashi
GONE!
大喜妙懲壞地主

Anna Fienberg
Barbara Fienberg 著

Kim Gamble 繪

王秋瑩 譯

三民書局

At four o'clock Jack met Tashi at the garden gate.

'Sorry I'm late,' **panted** Tashi, 'but three of our chickens **escaped** through a hole in the fence and we had to **chase** them to the creek and back. **Pesky** things!'

Tashi wiped his feet on the mat. Jack looked down curiously at Tashi's boots, and **sniffed**.

'Perhaps I'd better leave them outside,' said Tashi.

'Perhaps,' agreed Jack.

四點的時候，傑克和大喜在花園的大門口碰頭。

「對不起，我遲到了。」大喜氣喘吁吁地說，「我們有三隻雞從籬笆的破洞跑掉了，害我們得追到溪邊去，把牠們給追回來。真討厭！」

大喜在鞋墊上擦鞋子。傑克好奇地低頭瞧了瞧大喜的靴子，聞了一聞。「也許我最好把靴子放在外頭。」大喜說。

「也許吧。」傑克附和著。

pant [pænt] 動 氣喘吁吁地說

escape [ɪˋskep] 動 逃跑

chase [tʃes] 動 追捕

pesky [ˋpɛskɪ] 形 惱人的

sniff [snɪf] 動 用鼻子聞

'So,' said Jack, when they were sitting comfortably, 'did you get all three chickens back?'

'Oh yes,' said Tashi, 'but I remember a time when it wasn't so easy. Once, every hen in our village **disappeared**. Nothing was left behind— not even a **feather floating** in the air.'

'How **dreadful**,' said Mom, coming into the room. 'What did you do for eggs?'

'Well,' said Tashi, **stretching** out his legs, 'it was like this.'

「那麼，」當他們舒舒服服地坐下來的時候，傑克說，「你有把三隻雞全追回來嗎？」「噢，有啊，」大喜說，「不過我記得有一次事情可沒這麼容易。有一次，我們村裡的母雞全都不見了。什麼都沒剩——連根飄在空中的羽毛也沒有。」

「糟了，」老媽走進房間時說，「那你們要怎麼獲得雞蛋呢？」

「這個嘛，」大喜伸了伸腿說，「事情是這樣的。」

disappear [ˌdɪsəˈpɪr] 動 消失不見
feather [ˈfɛðɚ] 名 羽毛
float [flot] 動 飄浮
dreadful [ˈdrɛdfəl] 形 糟透了
stretch [strɛtʃ] 動 伸展

'Wait,' cried Jack. 'Dad's still **asleep**. Fair's fair.' He scrambled upstairs, **flung** open his father's door, and shouted 'BABA YAGA!' Dad screamed and shot out of bed as if the **witch** was **swooping** through the window right behind him.

He was still breathing heavily when he was settled on the sofa with a **rug** over his knees. He stared at Tashi. 'I don't know how you could even look at chickens again after Baba Yaga,' he said, and **sneezed**.

「等一下，」傑克喊著，「老爸還在睡覺。為公平起見。」他爬上樓去，啪地一聲打開老爸的房門，大叫一聲：「巴巴鴉加！」

老爸尖叫起來，衝下床，好似巫婆正穿過他後面的窗戶，朝他猛撲過來。

當老爸用條毯子蓋住膝蓋，坐定在沙發上的時候，他還是喘得很屬害呢。他盯著大喜看。邊打噴嚏邊說，「我不明白你在巴巴鴉加的事件之後怎麼還能看住雞。」

asleep [əˋslip] 形 睡著的

fling [flɪŋ] 動 猛然移動

witch [wɪtʃ] 名 女巫

swoop [swup] 動 突擊

rug [rʌg] 名 毛毯

sneeze [sniz] 動 打噴嚏

'Hmm,' Tashi nodded, 'but a man has to eat. When all the hens disappeared, no one in the village had a **clue** where they could be. People were **grizzling** because they had to start work without their **omelets**. They invented **excuses** to **poke** about in each other's houses, but they found nothing.

「嗯，」大喜點點頭，「可是人得要吃飯哪！當母雞
全都不見的時候，村民連一點雞在哪的線索都沒有。村
民嘟嘟嚷嚷地抱怨著，因為沒吃煎蛋捲就去上工。他們
想出各種藉口到別人家打探，不過都一無所獲。」

clue [klu] 名 線索
grizzle [`grɪzl̩] 動 （嘟嘟嚷嚷地）抱怨
omelet [`amlɪt] 名 煎蛋捲
excuse [ɪk`skjus] 名 藉口
poke [pok] 動 四處找，打探《about》

'One day my mother threw down her spoon
and said she was tired of trying to cook without
eggs. She sent me over to Third Aunt, who
worked as a cook for the **wicked** Baron. Since
he was the richest man in the village, she
thought that perhaps he might have a few eggs
left.'

「有一天，我老媽丟下她的湯匙說，她再也無法忍受煮菜時沒有雞蛋了。她派我去在壞地主家當廚子的三嬸那兒。媽媽想，既然大地主是村裡最有錢的人，他可能還有一些雞蛋才是。」

wicked [`wɪkəd] 形 壞的

'Oh I remember *him*!' cried Dad. 'He was that **rascal** who kept all his money on a mountain—'

'Guarded by a pack of white tigers,' shuddered Mom.

'Yes,' agreed Tashi. 'He had the heart of a robber, and the smile of a snake, and I didn't like going near him. But what else could I do? I set off at once and on the way I met Cousin Wu. He had just returned from a trip to the city, and he couldn't stop talking about the **wonders** he'd seen there. "The best thing of all," he said, "was the Flying Fireball Circus. You should have seen it, Tashi—the **jugglers** and the **acrobats** on the high **trapeze**—I couldn't believe my eyes."'

「哦，我記得他！」老爸叫了起來。「他就是那個把他所有的錢放在山上的惡棍——」

「由一群白老虎看管著。」老媽發著抖。

「沒錯，」大喜應和著。「他像強盜一樣黑心，像蛇一樣的笑臉，我不喜歡接近他。可是我還能怎麼辦呢？我馬上出發，半路上我遇見吳表弟。他剛從城市旅遊回來，不斷地說著他在那裡看到的不可思議的東西。『最棒的事，』他說，『就是那飛火球馬戲團了。你該去瞧一瞧，大喜——玩雜耍的和高空鞦韆的特技演員——我簡直不敢相信我的眼睛。』」

rascal [`ræskḷ] 名 惡棍，流氓

wonder [`wʌndɚ] 名 不可思議的東西

juggler [`dʒʌglɚ] 名 玩雜耍的人

acrobat [`ækrə,bæt] 名 特技演員

trapeze [træ`piz] 名 高空鞦韆

'"You are lucky, Wu," I sighed. "I don't suppose we will ever see a circus here. The village would never have enough money to pay for one to visit."'

'We walked along in silence for a while, and then I asked Cousin Wu if he wanted to come with me to the Baron's house.

Suddenly he seemed to be in a great hurry to visit his sister, so we said goodbye and I went on my way.

「『你好幸運哦，吳表弟。』我嘆了口氣，『我不認為我們會在這裡看到馬戲團。村子永遠不會有足夠的錢去請馬戲團來表演。』」

　　「我們倆靜靜地走了一會兒，然後我問吳表弟要不要跟我一塊兒去大地主家。

　　他突然好像急急忙忙要去看他姊姊，所以我們向對方說再見，而我就繼續往前走。

'**Unfortunately**, just as I was opening the gate
to the Baron's house, the wicked man himself
leant out the window and saw me. "Be off with
you, you little worm," he shouted. "I don't
want to see you **hanging about** my house!"'

「不湊巧的是，在我打開大地主家大門的時候，那壞蛋從窗戶探出身子，看到了我。『你這小蟲仔滾開，』他大吼，『我不想看見你在我的屋子周圍晃來晃去！』」

unfortunately [ˌʌnˋfɔrtʃənɪtlɪ] 副 不湊巧地
lean [lin] 動 探出身子（過去式leant [lɛnt]）
hang about 在…周圍徘徊

'Worm—*he's* the worm,' said Dad **crossly**. 'Someone ought to **squish** him!'

'Well,' Tashi went on, 'I **pretended** to run off home, but as soon as the Baron closed his shutters, I **ducked** back into the kitchen where Third Aunt had made some delicious sticky sweet rice cakes, my favourite. When I had **wolfed** down five or six, I remembered the eggs.

「蟲——他才是蟲呢！」老爸不悅地說。

「該有人去扁他一頓！」

「嗯，」大喜繼續說，「我假裝要跑回家，不過大地主一關上窗子，我就躲進廚房，在那三嬸做了我最愛吃的米糕，又黏又甜的。我狼吞虎嚥吃了五、六塊米糕之後，我才想起雞蛋的事。

crossly [`krɔslɪ] 副 不愉快地

squish [skwɪʃ] 動 輕輕地壓扁

pretend [prɪˋtɛnd] 動 假裝

duck [dʌk] 動 躲避

wolf [wʊlf] 動 狼吞虎嚥

'"Of course you can have some," said Third Aunt. "We have plenty. More than we know what to do with, in fact."

'"Have you?" I said. "That's very interesting." And I followed her outside to an **enormous shed** and waited while she **unlocked** the door. And do you know what? I found hundreds of hens—and some of them were my old friends! I **recognized** Gong Gong's **Pullet** and Second Cousin's big Peking Red.

『『你當然可以拿些雞蛋，』三嬸說，『我們有好多好多呢！其實，多到不知道該怎麼辦才好。』

　　『『是嗎？』我說，『很有意思哦。』我跟她走到外頭，來到一個很大的雞舍，等她開門鎖。

　　你們知道嗎？我看見好幾百隻母雞──其中有些是我的老朋友呢！我認出了剛剛的小母雞和二表哥的北京紅嘴大母雞。

enormous [ɪ`nɔrməs] 形 巨大的

shed [ʃɛd] 名 家畜棚

unlock [ʌn`lɑk] 動 開（門的）鎖

recognize [`rɛkəg,naɪz] 動 認出

pullet [`pʊlɪt] 名 小母雞

'"Don't wait for me," I told Third Aunt. "I'll fill
this bowl and be out **in a minute**." When she
left, I walked amongst the birds and made sure
that all the village hens were there in the
Baron's chicken house. Then I sniffed the smell
of **cigars**. Strange, I thought. Cigar smoke in a
chicken house? I sniffed again and the skin on
my neck **tingled**. Slowly I turned around. And
there, in the doorway **blocking** the light, stood
the wicked Baron.

「『別等我了，』我對三嬸說。『我要把蛋裝滿這個碗，等會兒再出去。』三嬸走了以後，我在雞群中走動，確定村子裡的母雞全在大地主的這個雞舍裡頭。接著我聞到了雪茄的味道。奇怪了，我心想。雞舍裡怎麼會有雪茄的味道？我又聞了聞，脖子上一陣刺痛。我慢慢地轉過身去。那壞地主就站在門口擋住了光線。

in a minute　立刻 (soon)
cigar [sɪˋgɑr]　名 雪茄
tingle [ˋtɪŋgl̩]　動 感到刺痛
block [blɑk]　動 擋住

23

'He **marched** inside and closed the door behind him. "So, little worms **wriggle** into **peculiar** places," he said with a **nasty sneer**. "But can they wriggle out again, I wonder?"

'"You have stolen all our chickens!" I cried. "Why? Whatever are you going to do with them?"

「他昂首闊步地走了進來，關上身後的門。『小蟲仔爬進這裡了，』他邊說邊發出令人討厭的冷笑，『不過我很懷疑牠們還能爬得出去嗎？』

　　『你偷了我們所有的雞！』我大喊，『怎麼樣？你打算把牠們怎樣？』」

march [mɑrtʃ] 動 昂首闊步地行走
wriggle [`rɪgl̩] 動 蠕動著前進
peculiar [pɪ`kjuljɚ] 形 特別的
nasty [`næstɪ] 形 討厭的
sneer [snɪr] 名 冷笑

'"That is none of your business...but then, maybe I'll tell you since you won't be here long enough to do anything about it." And he grinned, showing all his **glinting** gold teeth. "I am going to sell half of them to the River Pirate, who'll be sailing past this house at midnight. Then tomorrow, I'll be able to **charge** whatever I like for my eggs because no one else will have any to sell. I'll make a fortune! Golden eggs, they'll be! What do you think of that, little worm?"

'I stared at him. It was hard to believe anyone could be so mean.'

'I know,' agreed Dad, nodding his head. 'The newspapers are full of **crooks** getting away with it. Makes your blood boil.'

'Well, I was **determined** *he* wouldn't get away with it. I **edged** toward the door. "You can't keep me here," I told him, thinking I could make a dash for it.

『『這不干你的事⋯不過嘛，既然你不會在這裡太久而壞了我的好事，我就告訴你吧，』他咧嘴笑著，露出了閃閃發亮的金牙。『我打算把一半的母雞賣給河盜，他今晚半夜會划船經過這裡。然後明天，我就可以隨心所欲地開價賣我的雞蛋了，因為沒人會有雞蛋可以賣。我會大賺一筆！它們會是金雞蛋哪！你覺得怎麼樣啊，小蟲仔？』

「我瞪著他。很難相信會有人這麼壞。」

「我了解，」老爸點點頭表示同意。

「報紙上都是這些詐騙潛逃的騙子的事。教人熱血沸騰。」

「嗯，我決心不讓他得逞。我側身擠到門邊。『你不能把我關在這兒。』我邊說邊想要衝出去。

glint [glɪnt] 動 閃爍
charge [tʃɑrdʒ] 動 索價
crook [krʊk] 名 騙子
determine [dɪ`tɝmɪn] 動 決心
edge [ɛdʒ] 動 側著慢慢移動

27

'The Baron laughed **fiercely**. It sounded like a **growl**. "Oh no, little fish **bait**, I have plans for you. I will lock you up in the storeroom until midnight, when the River Pirate will take *you* as well as the hens. A pirate's **prisoner**, that's what you'll be!" And he **grabbed** me and threw me over his shoulder like a bit of old rope, and dropped me into the cold, dark storeroom.

「大地主大笑起來。聽起來像動物的咆哮聲。『噢，不，小魚餌，我有辦法對付你了。我要把你關在儲藏室，直到半夜河盜來把你跟母雞一起帶走。你會變成河盜的俘虜囉！』然後，他抓住我，像一串舊繩索般把我丟在他的肩膀上，然後扔進那又冷又黑的儲藏室。

fiercely [`fɪrslɪ] 副 激烈地
growl [graul] 名 咆哮
bait [bet] 名 誘餌
prisoner [`prɪzn̩ɚ] 名 犯人
grab [græb] 動 抓住

'At first, there was just darkness, and silence. But as my eyes grew used to the **gloom**, I saw the walls were thick stone, and a square of grey light shone in through one small high window. I felt all round the heavy iron door, but it was **padlocked**, as tight as a **treasure** chest. I **bent** down to study the floor, to see if there were any **trapdoors**, or loose stones. And it was then that I saw it. Lying in the corner, curled up like a wisp of smoke, was a white tiger.'

「起初，那兒又黑又安靜。不過在我的眼睛適應黑暗之後，我看見牆壁是厚厚的石頭，一塊灰色的光透過上面的一個小窗射進來。我摸遍了那又厚又重的鐵門，不過鐵門就像百寶箱一樣地鎖著。我彎下腰研究地板，看看是否有任何的活門或鬆動的石頭。就在這時候，我看到了牠。是一隻白老虎像一縷煙一樣地躺在角落，捲曲在那裡。

gloom [glum] 名 陰暗
padlock [`pæd͵lɑk] 動 以掛鎖鎖住
treasure [`trɛʒɚ] 名 寶藏
bend [bɛnd] 動 彎腰
trapdoor [`træp͵dɔr] 名 活門

'The Baron's tiger!' screamed Jack. 'What did you do?'

'Well, it was like this. I just stayed where I was and made no sound. I could see that its eyes were closed. Its legs **twitched** now and then, as if it were chasing something in a dream. It was asleep, but for how long? I put my head in my hands. There was no way out. I felt like a fly in a **web**. Only *my* web was made of solid stone. 'If only I had my **magic** ghost cakes, I thought. I could walk through that wall, as easily as walking through air. I searched in my empty pockets. Wait! There was a small **crumb**. But would it be enough to get me all the way through those thick walls? Should I **take the chance**?'

'Yes, yes!' cried Jack.

「大地主的老虎！」傑克尖叫了起來，「你要怎麼辦哪？」

「這個嘛，事情是這樣的。我待在原地不出聲。我看見牠的眼睛閉著。牠的腿偶爾抽動一下，好像牠在夢裡追趕什麼似的。牠睡著了，但是會睡多久呢？我把頭埋進了手裡。沒有辦法出去了。我覺得自己就像蜘蛛網上的蒼蠅。只不過我的網是用堅硬的石頭做的。

「我那時候想，如果我有神奇的鬼派，我就可以像穿過空氣那麼容易地穿過那道牆了。我摸了摸我那空空的口袋。等等！有塊小碎屑。但這夠讓我一路穿過那些厚厚的牆嗎？我該試試看嗎？」

「試呀，要試呀！」傑克大叫。

twitch [twɪtʃ] 動 抽動

web [wɛb] 名 網

magic [ˈmædʒɪk] 形 魔法般的

crumb [krʌm] 名 麵包屑

take the chance 試試看

Tashi nodded. 'I put the crumb on my tongue and as I **swallowed** I began to push through the stone. My right foot first—it was gliding through!—and then I stopped. The rest of my leg was **stuck fast**, deep inside the stone.

'I moaned aloud. Over my shoulder I saw the tiger **stir**. I saw one eye open. Then the other. I'd forgotten the color of those eyes: red, like coals of fire. The tiger growled deep in its throat. It made me think of the Baron, and how he would laugh to see me **trapped** like this. Slowly, lazily, the tiger uncurled itself.

大喜點點頭。「我把碎屑放在舌頭上，一邊吞、一邊開始要穿過石頭。首先是我的右腳——它滑過了！——然後我停住了。我的左腳緊緊地、深深地卡在石頭裡。

　　我大聲地呻吟。一轉頭，我看見老虎動了。我看見牠張開了一隻眼睛。接著是另一隻眼。我忘了牠眼睛的顏色：紅的，像炭火般地紅。老虎從喉嚨裡發出怒吼聲，這怒吼聲讓我想到了大地主，他如果看到我現在受困的樣子，會如何嘲笑我呢？

　　老虎慢慢地、懶懶地舒展自己。

swallow [`swɑlo] 勔 吞

stick [stɪk] 勔 卡住（過去分詞 stuck [stʌk]）

fast [fæst] 勔 牢固地

stir [stɝ] 勔 移動

trap [træp] 勔 使落入圈套

'I scrabbled through my top pockets. Nothing. I was **frantic**. The tiger was **padding** towards me. It **leaned** back **on its haunches**, ready to **spring**. It was hard to look away from its snarling mouth, but yes, there in the very last pocket of all, I felt something soft and **squashy**. Another cake crumb!

'I swallowed the crumb as the tiger sprang. Its
jaws opened and a **spiky whisker swiped** my
hand, but I was away, slipping through the stone
as easily as a fish noodle slips down your throat.

「我胡亂摸著我上面的口袋。空的！我快瘋了。老虎正無聲無息地走向我。牠往後蹲坐，準備要跳了。我很難不看牠那張咆哮的嘴，不過，有了，就在最後一個口袋，我摸到軟軟的、扁扁的東西。另一塊鬼派碎屑！

frantic [`fræntɪk] 形 發狂的

pad [pæd] 動 無聲無息地走

lean on one's haunch　蹲坐下來

spring [sprɪŋ] 動 跳

squashy [`skwaʃɪ] 形 易壓扁的

「就在老虎起跳的時候，我吞了那碎屑。牠張大了嘴巴，尖尖的鬍鬚擦過了我的手，不過我就像魚麵滑下喉嚨般那樣容易地穿過石頭逃開了。

jaw [dʒɔ] 名 顎
spiky [`spaɪkɪ] 形 尖的
whisker [`hwɪskɚ] 名 鬍鬚
swipe [swaɪp] 動 重擊

'Outside it was cool and **breezy**, and I stretched my arms out wide and did a little dance of freedom. Then I saw Cousin Wu, coming back from his sister's. I ran to him and told him, in a great rush, what the Baron had done.

'"That **thieving devil**!" cried Cousin Wu. "I'd like to drop him down a great black hole, down to the burning center of the earth! But first, let's go and tell the village."

'"You go," I said, "but just say to everyone that you've **discovered** who stole the hens—nothing more. There is something I have to do here first."'

「外頭涼涼的、又有微風，我伸開雙臂，為重獲自由手舞足蹈了一下。接著我看見吳表弟，從他姊姊那兒回來。我跑過去，一口氣把大地主幹的好事告訴他。

　　『那個像小偷一樣的壞蛋！』吳表弟大叫。『我真想把他丟到一個大黑洞裡，教他掉到燃燒的地心去！不過，我們先去告訴村子裡的人吧！』

　　『你去，』我說，『但是只要告訴大家，你已經發現偷雞的人是誰了——別的不用說。我要先在這裡做點事。』」

breezy [`brizɪ] 形 微風吹拂的
thieve [θiv] 動 作賊
devil [`dɛvl̩] 名 惡魔
discover [dɪ`skʌvɚ] 動 發現

'What?' cried Dad, **hanging on to** his blanket.
Tashi smiled. 'I had other plans for the Baron.
You see, it was almost midnight. I hurried
down to the Baron's **jetty**, to wait for the River
Pirate. The moon was up, and soon I heard the
soft *shush* *shush* of the **motor**. The boat came
around the **bend**, riding the moon's path of
silver. The Pirate tied up at the jetty, and
stepped out.

「甚麼？」老爸叫了起來，緊緊抓著毯子。

　　大喜笑了笑。「我有別的計畫對付大地主。你知道的，當時快半夜了。我衝到大地主的碼頭等河盜。月亮升了上來，不一會兒，我聽到有馬達發出輕輕的噓噓聲。船順著河面的銀色月光來到河彎。河盜在碼頭繫好了船，走了出來。

hang on to... 緊緊抓住…
jetty [`dʒɛtɪ] 名 碼頭
shush [ʃʌʃ] 感 噓聲
motor [`motɚ] 名 馬達
bend [bɛnd] 名 河彎

'He was tall and looked as strong as ten lions. I
didn't **fancy** being taken as his prisoner, but
still I went to meet him. "I have some news
from the Baron," I began. "He has **changed his
mind** about selling you the hens."

'The River Pirate **frowned**. It was a terrible

frown, and I **noticed** him stroke the **handle** of his **sword**. Quickly I added, "But I have something for you." I drew out of my pocket a small bag of "gold" that a **tricky** genie had given me some time ago. "The Baron said that this is for your trouble."

'Well, the River Pirate stopped frowning, and **clapped** me on the back.

「他好高大，看起來像十頭獅子那麼壯。我不敢想像做他的俘虜會怎樣，不過我還是走過去和他碰了頭。『大地主要我帶話給你，』我開始說，『他改意心意不想賣母雞給你了。』

「河盜皺了皺眉。樣子好可怕，

fancy [ˋfænsɪ] 勔 想像

change one's mind 改變主意

frown [fraun] 勔 皺眉頭

我注意到他抽了一下劍柄。很快地我又說，『不過我有個東西要給你。』我從口袋裡拿出一小袋『金子』，那是以前一個難纏的精靈給我的。『大地主說這算是彌補你的。』

　　「唔，河盜不再皺眉了，還拍了拍我的背。

notice [`notɪs] 動 注意到
handle [`hændl̩] 名 握柄
sword [sord] 名 劍
tricky [`trɪkɪ] 形 狡猾的
clap [klæp] 動 輕拍

'In the distance I could see a large crowd of people marching from the village. They were waving **flaming torches** high above their heads, shouting fiercely. And there was the Baron coming out of his house, on his way down to meet the River Pirate. He hurried over to see what all the smoke and noise was about, and when he saw me, he **gasped** with surprise.

'I walked up to him and said **sternly**, "Here come the villagers. Can you see how angry they are? How **furious**? You have two **choices**. Either I will tell them how you stole their hens—and who knows what they will do to you, with their flaming torches and **fiery tempers**." The Baron turned pale in the moonlight.

'"Or?" he asked. "What about the *or*?"

「遠遠地我看見一大群人從村子走來。他們高高地揮舞著火把，激烈地大叫著。大地主正好從他的房子走出來，要去跟河盜碰面。他趕忙過去瞧瞧那些煙和吵鬧聲是怎麼回事，當他看見了我，驚訝得喘不過氣來。

flaming [`flemɪŋ] 形 燃燒的
torch [tɔrtʃ] 名 火把
gasp [gæsp] 動 透不過氣

「我向他走去，嚴肅地說，『村民來了。你看他們多生氣？多憤怒？你有兩個選擇。一個是我告訴他們你怎麼偷了他們的母雞——沒人知道他們會怎麼用他們燃燒的火把和憤怒來對付你。』大地主的臉在月光下變得蒼白起來。

　　『另一個呢？』他問，『另一個怎樣？』

sternly [`stɝnlɪ] 副 嚴肅的
furious [`fjʊrɪəs] 形 憤怒的
choice [tʃɔɪs] 名 選擇
fiery [`faɪrɪ] 形 易怒的
temper [`tɛmpɚ] 名 火氣

'"Or," I said slowly, stretching out the word like a **rubbery** noodle, "I can tell them you discovered that the River Pirate had stolen their hens, and, as an act of **kindness**, you bought the hens back for them."

'The Baron gave a great growl of **relief**. "That's the one I like, Tashi, my boy!"

'But I hadn't finished. "And you will invite them all to see the wonderful Flying Fireball Circus, which you will bring here to the village next week."

'"The circus? Are you mad? You **sneaky** little worm, that would cost me a fortune!" roared the Baron.

'"Yes," I agreed. "Don't those flames look **splendid** against the black sky?"

'And when the Baron turned to see, the villagers were almost upon us. "WHERE IS THE THIEF! WHERE IS THE THIEF!" they chanted.'

「『另一個，』我慢慢地，像一根有彈性的麵條把話拉長地說，『我可以告訴他們你發現河盜偷了他們的母雞，而且好心地把母雞買回來給他們。』

「大地主大大地鬆了一口氣。

『我喜歡這個，大喜，乖小子！』

「我還沒說完。『下星期你把飛火球馬戲團帶到村子來，請村民去觀賞他們精彩的表演。』

「『馬戲團？你瘋了？你這陰險的小蟲仔，這要花我很多錢吧！』大地主怒吼起來。

「『是啊！』我知道。『那些火焰在夜空下看起來是不是很壯觀啊？』

「當大地主回頭看的時候，村民幾乎快到了，重覆喊著，『小偷在哪裡！小偷在哪裡！』」

rubbery [ˋrʌbərɪ] 形 有彈性的
kindness [ˋkaɪndnɪs] 名 好意
relief [rɪˋlif] 名 （痛苦、憂慮等的）減輕
sneaky [ˋsnikɪ] 形 陰險的
splendid [ˋsplɛndɪd] 形 壯麗的

'And did the villagers set upon him with their fiery tempers?' Dad asked **eagerly**.

'No,' Tashi smiled. 'We all went to see the acrobats and the jugglers and the **daredevil horsemen** at the circus, and we had the best night of our lives.'

「村民有對他發洩他們的怒氣嗎？」老爸迫不及待地問。

　　「沒有，」大喜笑了笑，「我們全都去看馬戲團的特技演員、雜耍演員和膽大的騎師，度過了我們生平最美好的一晚。」

eagerly [`igəlɪ] 副 急切地
daredevil [`dɛr͵dɛvḷ] 名 蠻勇的人
horseman [`hɔrsmən] 名 馬術師

'So,' Dad sighed, 'I suppose everyone had eggs for breakfast from then on and talked about the circus over tea, and Cousin Wu saw a lot of his sister.'

'Yes,' agreed Tashi, 'life was quite **peaceful**—for a while. Hey, Jack,' Tashi turned to his friend, 'let's go out into the garden and play Baba Yaga.'

'Okay,' said Jack. 'I'll be the witch and you can be the dinner,' and they **raced** outside to the **peppercorn** tree.

Dad went back to bed.

「那麼，」老爸嘆了一口氣，「我想從此大家早餐都有蛋吃了，喝茶時則談論馬戲團的事，而吳表弟也常去看他姐姐囉！」

　　「沒錯，」大喜說，「生活是平靜了點——持續了一陣子。嗨，傑克！」大喜轉過身對他朋友說，「我們去花園裡玩扮巴巴鴉加吧！」

　　「好啊，」傑克說，「我來當巫婆，你來當晚餐。」他們倆跑到外頭的黑胡椒樹下去了。

　　老爸則回去睡覺了。

peaceful [`pisfəl] 形 平靜的
race [res] 動 跑；賽跑
peppercorn [`pɛpɚ͵kɔrn] 名 黑胡椒

精心規劃，內容詳盡
三民英文辭典系列
學習英文的最佳輔助工具

三民皇冠英漢辭典（革新版）

大學教授、中學老師一致肯定、推薦，最適合中學生和英語初學者使用的實用辭典！

◎ 明顯標示國中生必學的507個單字和最常犯的錯誤，詳細、淺顯、易懂！
◎ 收錄豐富詞條及例句，幫助您輕鬆閱讀課外讀物！
◎ 詳盡的「參考」及「印象」欄，讓您體會英語的「弦外之音」！
◎ 賞心悅目的雙色印刷及趣味橫生的插圖，讓查辭典成為一大享受！！

三民新知英漢辭典

一本很生活、很實用的英漢辭典，讓您在生動、新穎的解說中快樂學習！

◎收錄中學、大專所需詞彙43,000字，總詞目多達60,000項。
◎增列「同義字圖表」，使同義字字義及用法差異在圖解說明下，一目了然。
◎加強重要字彙多義性的「用法指引」，充份掌握主要用法及用例。
◎雙色印刷，編排醒目，插圖生動靈活，輔助理解字義。

中學生．大專生適用

多種選擇，多種編寫設計
三民英文辭典系列
最能符合你的需要

三民精解英漢辭典（革新版）

一本真正賞心悅目，趣味橫生的英漢辭典誕生了！
雙色印刷＋漫畫式插圖，保證讓您愛不釋手！

◎收錄詞條25,000字，以中學生、社會人士常用詞彙為主。
◎常用基本字彙以較大字體標示，並搭配豐富的使用範例。
◎以五大句型為基礎，讓您更容易活用動詞型態。
◎豐富的漫畫式插圖，讓您在快樂的氣氛中學習，促進學習
　效率。
◎以圖框對句法結構、語法加以詳盡解說。

三民新英漢辭典（增訂完美版）

◎收錄詞目增至67,500項（詞條增至46,000項）。
◎新增「搭配」欄，羅列常用詞語間的組合關係，讓您掌
　握英語的慣用搭配，說出道地的英語。
◎詳列原義、引申義、確實掌握字詞釋義，加強英語字彙
　的活用能力。
◎附有精美插圖千餘幅，輔助詞義理解。
◎附錄包括詳盡的「英文文法總整理」、「發音要領解
　說」，提升學習效率。
◎雙色印刷，並附彩色英美地圖及世界地圖。

最有趣的英語讀本
最豐富的題材內容

探索英文叢書

是青少年朋友最佳的外語學習讀物

·中高級系列·

我家中樂透 (附CD)

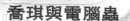

國王的試吃官 (附CD)
文建會「好書大家讀」活動推薦

喬琪與電腦蟲
文建會「好書大家讀」活動推薦

國家圖書館出版品預行編目資料

大喜妙懲壞地主／Anna Fienberg,Barbara Fienberg
　著;Kim Gamble繪;王秋瑩譯.－－初版一刷.－－臺
北市；三民，民90
　　面;公分－－(探索英文叢書.大喜說故事系列;10)
中英對照
ISBN 957-14-3420-5　(平裝)

　1.英國語言—讀本

805.18　　　　　　　　　　　　90002918

網路書店位址　http://www.sanmin.com.tw

© 　大喜妙懲壞地主

著作人　Anna Fienberg　Barbara Fienberg
繪　圖　Kim Gamble
譯　者　王秋瑩
發行人　劉振強
著作財　三民書局股份有限公司
產權人　臺北市復興北路三八六號
發行所　三民書局股份有限公司
　　　　地址／臺北市復興北路三八六號
　　　　電話／二五○○六六○○
　　　　郵撥／○○○九九九八——五號
印刷所　三民書局股份有限公司
門市部　復北店／臺北市復興北路三八六號
　　　　重南店／臺北市重慶南路一段六十一號
初版一刷　中華民國九十年四月
編　　號　S 85588
定　　價　新臺幣壹佰柒拾元
行政院新聞局登記證局版臺業字第○二○○號

有著作權·不准侵害

ISBN　957-14-3420-5　(平裝)